Spice Secret
A Teen's Cautionary Diary

BILLIE HOLLADAY SKELLEY, RN, MS

Spice Secret: A Teen's Cautionary Diary
Copyright © 2017 - 2025 by Billie Holladay Skelley, RN, MS
Originally Published 2017 by Goldminds Publishing, LLC (Hendersonville, TN) -Imprint of Amphorae Publishing (St. Louis, MO)

This is a work of fiction. Names, places, characters and incidents are either the product of the author's imagination or are used fictitiously, and any resemblance to any actual persons, living or dead, businesses, organizations, events or locales is entirely coincidental.

No part of this book may be reproduced or transmitted in any form or by any means, electronic or mechanical, including photocopying, recording, or by any information storage and retrieval system, without permission in writing from the author.

Library of Congress Control Number: 2025922646
ISBN: 978-1-959489-07-8

Cover design by Sharon Kizziah-Holmes

Published by

Crossing Time Press
Joplin, Missouri
Printed in the United States of America

For: *Desda Beatrice Meece Adams*

Table of Contents

Entry # 1: *It's a Wonderful Life* 1
   or   How Innocent Conversations Can Have Profound Consequences

Entry # 2: *Iron Man* 9
   or   How You Shouldn't Believe Everything You See in the Movies

Entry # 3: *Romeo and Juliet* 14
   or   How You Can't Judge a Book by Its Cover

Entry # 4: *Deep Impact* 18
   or   How You Should Not Bite Off More than You Can Chew

Entry # 5: *The Secret Garden* 23
   or   How Weeds Have Mastered Survival Skills

Entry # 6: *The Innocents Abroad* 32
   or   How You Can Go Wrong and Not Even Know It

Entry # 7: *Now You See Me* 38
   or   How Sometimes You Can't See What's Right in Front of Your Face

Entry # 8: *The Silence of the Lambs* 48
   or   How a Secret Can Be Kept from Others in the Hope of Keeping It from Yourself

Entry # 9: *Saturday Night Fever* 60
   or   How Cupid Can Misfire and Hit You in the Head Instead of the Heart

Entry # 10: *Fast and Furious* 65
   or   How in the Blink of an Eye You Can Lose Everything

Entry # 11: *Awakenings* 70
   or   How to Climb Out of a Black Hole

Entry # 12: *Back to the Future* 74
   or   How When You're on a Journey, You Should Look Back to See How Far You've Come

I am writing this for myself. If you want to read it that is fine, but I feel like I have to write it down just so I can remember how it happened. I know I will never forget certain things, but sometimes writing events down helps you to understand them better. It is a story that is difficult for me to tell, but I know it needs to be told.

Entry # 1:

It's a Wonderful Life

or

How Innocent Conversations Can Have Profound Consequences

I have a therapist. She asked me to keep this diary for twelve weeks to help me sort out my thoughts regarding what happened. I don't know if it will help, but I promised her I would try. I'm going to make one entry each week—as I think back about how it all went down.

I think the beginning—the real beginning—started with just a simple conversation with my best friend. I'll start here, but I may have to backtrack a little to explain our friendship. Anyway, here goes nothing……

"It's a strange and funny world."

"Is that more of your 'sage' advice?" I ask my friend.

Sage smirks good-naturedly at me and rolls her eyes. She disregards my attempt at humor. She's heard my pun response to her given name many times before.

"No, I think I heard it in a song on the radio," Sage answers with a grin. "It was a country song."

"So I'm supposed to follow the advice of a country singer?"

"No, Pepper, but sometimes it does seem like a strange and funny world. Maybe country singers know more about the world than we do."

"Oh, brother, it's come to this. I'm getting curriculum advice from the radio. Tell me what you think."

"I just think it is strange and kind of funny that

'Physical Education' and 'Great Books' are offered at the same time."

Sage is my best friend and my personal "sage"—pun intended. She is always giving me advice and offering guidance—even if it isn't profound or learned from years of experience. I know I can trust her, but her recommendations often come from country music or science fiction sources—two things she loves.

I remember, in that particular conversation, I was hoping to learn what classes she thought we should take for our junior year of high school. We were trying to prepare for college —you know, by taking a college-preparatory curriculum. It was just an innocent conversation, one of our usual back-and-forth banters, but in retrospect, it was the beginning. Neither of us had any idea, at the time, where the consequences of that class choice would lead.

Sage's full name is Sage Marie O'Dea. Why would anyone name their kid after a spice or herb? I don't know, and I should because my name is Pepper—Pepper Leann Kelly. Sage and I became friends partly because of our names. Before you laugh, remember friendships have been based on stranger things. Besides, I think names are important. They have far-reaching effects. Parents should probably think about this more when they choose names like Jurassic Park, Chris P. Bacon, and Bud Light for their offspring!

Sage and I met in grade school, and we immediately hit it off when we realized both of our names were spices. Okay, technically, I know that sage is an herb, but it is used like a spice. With that technicality bridged, Sage and I had no trouble cementing our relationship based on our names.

In the ensuing years, we've heard all the spice quips you can imagine —everything from little girls are made of "sugar and spice and everything nice" to "variety is the spice of life" —including every possible reference regarding the female British pop group, The Spice Girls. There were also the common spins, like "Oh, here are Pepper and Sage, they'll spice up the conversation" or "Here come Sage and Pepper, my favorite blend of spices." Every joke or word-play you can imagine regarding the word spice, I'm sure we've heard it.

Some of it, admittedly, we brought on ourselves. I remember, in grade school, the two of us actually did a poster board project on spices from A to Z—everything from allspice to zaatar. We tried to cover every spice we could find. We thought it was interesting, but, of course, our class was bored to tears.

Then there was our famous "spice bump." You know how athletes will fist pump or high five each other with "Good job" or "Go team." Well, Sage and I had this strange combination of a high five, then a fist-pump tap where we yelled "Spice Spirit!" It was somewhat short-lived—buried by ridicule I'm afraid to say, but we liked it. Looking back, I can understand how our signature move might have been perceived as somewhere between dorky and crazy, but I'm sure most people did dorky and crazy things in grade school.

In middle school, our enthusiasm for spices was not really curtailed, but we hid it better. Sage read Frank Herbert's science-fiction book, *Dune*, about "He who controls the spice, controls the universe," or something like that (I saw the movie). More than in science fiction (which I repeat Sage loves), we learned at school and at church about how important spices really have been in history. Do you remember the Spice Trade you learned about in school and how spices were an essential part of ancient commerce? They were used for everything from making perfume to embalming the dead. Spices were valuable commodities in the Bible, too. The Queen of Sheba gave spices to King Solomon, and the body of Jesus was bound in linen wrappings with spices. See, spices have been and are important!

Sage and I used to joke in sixth grade that if we were Italian, we could say we were Italian spices. We aren't, however, Italian. We are both of Irish descent, but it just sounded wrong to say Irish spices. Besides, we weren't sure what spices were used in Ireland anyway. We actually know very little about Ireland or any other place really because we have been marooned our whole lives in a small town in southwest Missouri.

In the ensuing years, however, we have gotten older and wiser. Well, I know we are older at least, and we've learned to keep a lower profile. Besides, most people in our school and in our town know us by now. That's one benefit of living in a small town—everybody knows everybody.

The downside of living in a small town is that everybody knows everybody. There are no secrets here. The other downside is there is not much to do. Our lives revolve around either church or school activities—and in our school, whether you are really into it or not, school revolves around football. Friday-night lights, meeting on the gridiron, tearing down the goalposts—you know, the drill. As juniors in high school, Sage and I went to all the football games, too—and that is where I first met Jordan.

Entry # 2:

Iron Man

or

How You Shouldn't Believe Everything You See in the Movies

"You're Pepper, aren't you?"

Those were his first words. It was early September, and a football game had just finished. Sage and I were walking across the field to go home, and Jordan was picking up a helmet left on the grass.

I remember feeling startled. I didn't know Jordan even knew my name. We did have one class together, "Great Books in English Literature" (Sage and I had finally selected "Great Books" because we concluded it would be more meaningful than PE, and neither of us particularly liked getting dressed out and showering for PE in the middle of the day). Evidently, Jordan was looking for meaning, too, because he was also in the class. Since Sage and I always sat in the back of the classroom, I didn't think Jordan knew I was even there, but finding my voice, I answered.

"Yes, I'm Pepper. Pepper Kelly."

"I remember you from class," Jordan continued, "because I heard your name was Pepper, and you reminded me of Pepper Potts."

"Pepper who?" I asked.

"Pepper Potts, you know, from the movie *Iron Man*."

I remember my mind racing to visualize the character in the movie. I had seen *Iron Man*. I mean we may live in the middle of nowhere, but we do have a movie theater. Then my brain brought up an image of Gwyneth Paltrow. She was pretty, very pretty, but

I wasn't sure if that was who he meant.

"You mean…Gwyneth Paltrow?" I asked.

"Yeah, you look like her," Jordan said, and he smiled again.

I smiled back, and that was it. With the helmet in his hand, Jordan turned and ran toward the locker room. Sage and I went home.

Jordan was a new student in our school, although there was technically nothing new about him. He looked like many of the other football players on our team. I mean he was cute—tall and muscular—but all I really knew about him was that he was from some other small town in Missouri. He had sat out of football for a year because of some problem or something. He transferred to our school for his senior year because our school had a reputation for having a good football program, and Jordan hoped to get a scholarship to play college football.

That first night, when he turned and ran off toward the locker room, I thought that would be it: just a greeting—an introduction—an acknowledgement that we both resided on the same planet. The following Monday, however, he talked to me after our "Great Books" class. Every day that week, after class, we talked a little more. A week later he called, and before long we were going out.

To this day, I don't know how Jordan originally got my phone number. Maybe he asked one of my friends. It doesn't really matter, because in a small town, it is not hard to find out someone's address or phone number.

To be honest, I am still not exactly sure what it was about him that caught my interest and why things progressed so fast. Maybe it was the flattery of being compared to a movie star or maybe it was just something new to do, I don't know, but soon Jordan and I were a couple.

Entry # 3:

Romeo and Juliet

or

How You Can't Judge a Book by Its Cover

"Pepper, do you want to hang out Friday night?" Sage asked.

"Sorry, I can't. Jordan is taking me to a movie."

In one form or another that exchange occurred more and more often as my relationship with Jordan grew. Jordan and I went to the movies, to school dances, out to eat, and of course, to football games. We even went to church on a few Sunday mornings. He was interesting to talk to and fun to be around. Sometimes we just hung out together and did nothing, but it was nice.

I remember realizing, at one point, that all of this new "boyfriend" activity with Jordan was taking time away from my schoolwork, but I decided I could manage. What I really felt bad about, during this period, was that our relationship also took away from the time I could spend with Sage. I saw less and less of her. As my friend, I know she understood, but I still felt bad about it.

Fortunately, Jordan had a "semi-good" friend on the football team, Dillon, and sometimes the four of us hung out together. On one of these occasions (maybe it was in early November, I can't remember exactly now), I noticed Sage seemed to really like Dillon. I, however, was not so sure about him. We had known Dillon casually for years, but he hadn't lit up our radar screens often. I guess you could say, previously, we just sort of knew him in passing. From my perspective, Sage and Dillon seemed like opposites.

You see, since the beginning of high school, Sage

and I had employed this strategy of doing everything we possibly could to get into college—so we could get away from small-town living. Remember that college-prep curriculum I mentioned? Sage and I knew it was important to build up the ol' CV, too. All those empty little boxes on college entrance forms have to be filled in with something. We tried clubs, student government, sports, and any other activity we thought we could manage.

Dillon, on the other hand, didn't seem to me to be very "high" on high school. (In retrospect, who is really?) What I mean is, Dillon didn't do anything, except football. He was good at that, I know, because his name was always in the paper for some scoring feat, but I don't think he was involved in anything else. He never talked about college or his future plans. If you asked him, he always said he was staying loose and keeping his options open. I guess maybe I thought he was sort of a loner and not really planning for the future. Don't get me wrong, because like I said, Dillon had always been nice enough, it's just he gave off the impression of kind of hearing his own drummer. Maybe that is a good thing—to hear your own drummer—I don't know. I can't explain it very well, but at the time, I thought Dillon was just the opposite of Sage. He was also the opposite of Jordan, who was always so earnest, hardworking, involved, and focused on getting into college.

I remember mentioning this back then to Sage, and in her "sage" voice, she said, "You know, Pepper, you can't judge a book by its cover."

She was right of course. Sage is always right.

Anyway, Jordan and I began to spend a lot of time together. I liked him. I really liked him. I felt like I could trust Jordan. Then one afternoon, out of nowhere, it happened.

Entry # 4:

Deep Impact
or
How You Should Not Bite Off More than You Can Chew

"You need to tell me," I said, "when you want me to have the food ready and where you want me to put it."

I was talking to Dallas Freeman, the president of our junior class and also the president of the student council. We were having an informal meeting on the front steps of the school about our upcoming Fall Festival. The junior class puts it on every year, and as a member of the Junior Class Spirit Committee, I needed to know what the schedule was and what we needed to do to get ready. There were other committee members there, too.

"Everything goes in the cafeteria," Dallas responded. "If it starts at seven, I guess everything should be there and ready by six-thirty."

It was Wednesday, November 18th. I remember because the Fall Festival was the following Friday. The whole discussion was just about the refreshments and decorations. It was just simple things like that. We were laughing and goofing around, but it didn't mean anything. I have known Dallas since kindergarten. He is just a friend—but one who is involved in many activities, too.

Jordan was waiting for me in his truck and watching our interaction on the steps. When I finished and joined Jordan, I noticed he looked upset. I asked him what was wrong, and he said he didn't want to talk about it. He said we would talk about it later.

We left school in Jordan's truck, and he didn't say a word while we drove out to County Road 128. I couldn't imagine what was wrong, but he stopped suddenly, got out of the truck, and started to walk across a field dotted with large, round hay bales. I called to him and ran to catch up with him. When I reached him, he turned, and I saw his face. He was livid. His cheeks were red, and his eyes were blazing. I had never seen anyone so mad.

Before I knew what had happened, Jordan slapped me hard across the cheek. Caught completely off guard, I stumbled backwards toward one of the hay bales. My hand went instinctively to my face. My cheek was stinging.

"What was that for? What's wrong with you?" I asked.

"There's nothing wrong with me. There's something wrong with you," Jordan yelled between clenched teeth. "You know what it's for."

"No, I don't. I don't have any idea. What are you talking about? What's wrong with me?"

"You disrespected me in front of all those people... smiling and flirting with Dallas Freeman. He's a weak-kneed nerd, and you were purposely trying to make me jealous."

I couldn't believe my ears. I hadn't flirted with Dallas. I have never wanted to flirt with Dallas. I like him—we have been friends forever—but just friends. I never dated Dallas and never wanted to date him. There was nothing there.

I told all that to Jordan. I repeated it over and over. I told him Dallas and I were just talking. We were both on the committee planning the festival. It was just talk—no flirting—no desire to flirt. I remember it took at least an hour, maybe longer, but Jordan eventually calmed down.

For a while, we just stood there. Then, tightly holding me in his arms, Jordan finally spoke. His voice was almost a whisper.

"I'm sorry. I didn't mean to hit you. It's just that you made me so mad, I couldn't help it. Promise me you'll never do that again."

He was holding me so tightly that I promised. I mean I wanted to promise—even though I didn't know really what I had done. I just knew I didn't want it to happen ever again. I told Jordan that. He assured me it wouldn't and repeated that he was sorry. There were tears in his eyes. I know he really was sorry.

Entry # 5:

The Secret Garden

or

How Weeds Have Mastered Survival Skills

I've always hated conflict. I mean I try to avoid physical confrontation if at all possible. It has just always seemed to me there ought to be more civilized ways to deal with problems. If people can talk and really communicate, they should be able to solve problems without resorting to physical violence. The attack from Jordan was just foreign to me. I didn't understand it, and I couldn't explain it.

The result was that I didn't tell anyone what had happened—not even Sage. Maybe I was embarrassed.

I don't know, but I convinced myself I could handle it. There was really no harm done after all. It was just a misunderstanding, and I didn't feel it was necessary to discuss it again. No one else needed to know.

Anyway, I didn't want Jordan to look bad in the eyes of other people. I thought, since it only affected me, it would just be my secret. People keep lots of secrets. Besides, Jordan might be upset if he thought I was talking about him behind his back.

I rationalized the whole incident in the hayfield was just a fluke. Everyone knows people have bad days, and all relationships have their ups and downs. That day was just one of the downs. It was just one of those things that happened, and then you forget about it.

Jordan and I didn't talk about what happened that day either. There was no need to discuss it. He was as sweet, attentive, and caring as he had ever been—maybe more so. He really was sorry. That day in the hayfield was just a weird one. The stars had been out of alignment or something.

That's not to say Jordan didn't have a temper. Everyone does, but I found that certain things could set him off. I mean one time he got really mad at one of the guys on the football team for calling him a "jock." The guy didn't mean anything by it, but Jordan didn't like it. There wasn't a fight or anything, but Jordan's face turned red, and he clinched his teeth so hard I could hear them grinding. I thought, like me, he was just extremely sensitive to labels.

I don't like labels. I know this probably is hard to believe coming from the "spice" girl, but I think it's bad to label or pigeon-hole people. People are way too complicated for that. Besides, Jordan was much more than just an athlete. He was a good student, he loved music, and he did all kinds of community service. He said the community service was part of his push to get into a good college, but he did it—and I think he enjoyed it.

Anyway, the school year moved on, and so did the football season. Before long it was time for Thanksgiving and Christmas, and both of those holidays turned out to be wonderful. Jordan had dinner with my family on both occasions, and everyone liked him. I gave him an authentic Kansas City Chiefs sweatshirt for Christmas, and he gave me a beautiful blue topaz necklace. I loved the necklace and wore it almost every day. Unfortunately, the holidays passed quickly, and before anyone was ready, it was January again, and we were returning to school.

Many of our classes changed with the new semester, but some were year-long endeavors. I was glad for these courses, especially "Great Books," because it was then that I mostly saw Sage. She was still seeing Dillon. I continued to have some concerns about Dillon, but if he made Sage happy, why should I voice any doubts about him? Besides, maybe back then, Sage had doubts about Jordan, but she never said anything negative about him to me. She knew Jordan made me happy.

When Jordan and I were together, it was great. We both liked to exercise, and we ran, took hikes, and biked. When he worked out in the gym lifting weights, I walked on the treadmill. We even liked studying together and discussing possible scenarios for college. It would be nice, we concluded, if we could go to the same college. We enjoyed our time together. It was special. I especially enjoyed taking him to visit places that were new to him, but that I had known all my life—like coffee shops, pizza parlors, and nature centers. It was so much better to be with him than to be without him.

When we were apart, Jordan always wanted to know where I had been, what I was doing, and who had been there. He was attentive and protective like that. Not often, but sometimes, he seemed a little overprotective.

I remember one Sunday afternoon in early January, when I had plans to meet up with Sage after church, Jordan insisted on coming along. I told him we weren't really going to be doing anything, just hanging out, but he was persistent. He really wanted to come.

"Why is it so important to you to see Sage?" I asked him.

"It's not that I want to see Sage," he answered.

"Then what is it?" I asked. "Surely you don't want to hang out all afternoon listening to spicy girl talk."

Jordan looked worried. He just stared at me. I didn't like his look.

"What is it, Jordan?" I asked more seriously. "What are you worried about?"

He didn't answer at first. He just rubbed his palms

together and looked closely at his hands. Finally, he spoke.

"I know how close you and Sage are, and I guess I'm a little jealous," he said. His eyes moved from his hands to my face. "I know how girls like to talk, and I'm afraid…I'm worried that you might say something… about what happened in the hayfield."

I had totally repressed the whole hayfield incident. It was just a fluke, remember?

"Jordan, honestly," I said in my most reassuring voice, "I have never said anything to anyone about that day—not even Sage. I've totally forgotten about it. Please believe me."

I remember feeling relieved that I had kept the whole thing a secret so I could honestly tell him I hadn't told anyone anything.

Jordan seemed pleased that I had kept the incident a secret, but he remained worried about my scheduled visit with Sage. In the end, when my repeated reassurances failed to convince him that everything was okay, I decided it was easier to just cancel with Sage. I spent the afternoon instead with Jordan, and he seemed really happy to have me with him.

One other time, I remember, occurred when we went out to eat at a local restaurant. I got up to go to the restroom, and I left my purse in the seat. When I was coming back to the table, I thought I saw Jordan looking at my cell phone.

"What are you doing?" I asked, looking at my phone and purse. Jordan seemed startled at the question.

"I was…I was just looking for some gum. I thought you might have a piece."

"Why did you have my phone?" I asked more directly.

"I just picked it out of your purse to look for the gum. Is anything the matter?"

I didn't know. I mean it looked kind of weird, but his explanation sounded plausible. It really didn't matter to me anyway. I mean I'd let him see or use my phone anytime—so, in the end, I just told him that nothing was the matter and everything was fine.

Excluding those two rather strange encounters, dating Jordan was wonderful. He was a great boyfriend—smart, attractive, and considerate. Life was good, and my junior year of high school seemed to be turning out better than I could have planned. It was also flying by.

Entry # 6:

The Innocents Abroad

or

How You Can Go Wrong and Not Even Know it

In mid-January, the Spirit Committee began making plans for our annual Valentine's Day Dance. We decided this year's theme would be Cupid's Party Night. It was not a very original theme, but it was short and to the point.

As class president and head of the student council, Dallas Freeman was very involved with the Spirit Committee. After the fireworks he had generated previously, however, I decided, long before our scheduled committee meetings, I would steer clear of him. I didn't want to be paired with him for some assignment and have Jordan think I intentionally selected Dallas out for an activity or interaction. I felt it was best—for everyone concerned—to stay away from Dallas.

During our first meeting to prepare for Cupid's Party Night, I tried to lay low and not volunteer for any big task. With all my schoolwork, church activities, and Jordan, I was too busy to take on much anyway. In the end, the only job I got, along with Adam Ansley, was to find a Cupid statue so we could have a "Selfie Station" where couples could take pictures with Cupid—the god of desire, affection, and love.

Adam and I searched everywhere in our area for Cupid statues, and it might come as no surprise to you, but in a small town, statues of Cupid are not in abundance. After several phone calls, we finally found a florist about forty-five miles from our school that had recently acquired a new Cupid statue. They were willing to loan us their old one, if we promised its safe return. Adam and I made plans to retrieve it on Saturday—a week before the scheduled Cupid's Party Night dance.

Early that Saturday morning, Adam arrived at my house with his pickup truck. I had gathered up several old blankets and comforters to use for padding to cushion the statue in the truck. With roughly about an hour's drive to get there, including the time required to position and pad the statue, and the return trip, I figured we should be back in town and at the school by noon. I told Jordan this because I wanted him to know that I would be back in plenty of time for a date we had planned for that night. We were going to a movie.

Adam and I arrived at the florist without any problems. The people that worked there were nice, but their statue turned out to be much larger and heavier than we'd anticipated. Their version of the winged hero stood over six-feet tall! He had one arm raised high in the air, and he held a long, slender bow in his opposite hand that looked ready for his arrows. I was glad I had brought the blankets for padding because this particular example of the "god of love" seemed to have a lot of potentially breakable appendages.

Worried that we might crack him or even worse break something off, we tried to cover and pad everything as best we could. Of course, this made the statue even more difficult to move and more awkward to maneuver. Under the watchful eyes of the owners of the florist, it was stressful work, but we did our best to be careful. Fortunately, a young man, who made deliveries for the florist, offered to help us lift and position our carefully-wrapped archer. It was slow going, but by noon, we had Cupid comfortably reclining in the bed of the truck.

Adam and I started on our way, but we hadn't gone twenty miles when his truck had a flat tire on the right rear side. Adam had a spare, but it took some time to get to it, and the damaged tire didn't seem to want to come off at first. When Adam tried to put the spare on, Cupid rocked and tilted with every movement of the jack. We were both afraid the huge, arrow-toting man with wings was going to chip or crack. Adam tried to be careful, but again, it was slow going. Finally, the spare was on, and by two o'clock, we were on the road again. Adam and I joked about how we should have brought more people along to help move this hefty lover boy or to at least help with the flat.

We decided the best course was to take the statue directly to the school so we could get help unloading it. Fortunately, when we arrived, the basketball team was taking a break from a Saturday practice, and they helped us unload our Cupid and move him to a corner of the gym. It was almost four o'clock by the time the statue was safely set up and I had retrieved my blankets and comforters. I left school later than I'd planned, but relieved we'd succeeded in getting Cupid ready for the dance.

I hurried home to eat and do some schoolwork. I also wanted to get ready for my date with Jordan. It meant rushing some, but I knew, if I hustled, I could get everything done.

Jordan arrived about seven in the evening, and we left for the theater. He seemed a little reserved, but he did ask about our trip to retrieve Cupid. I told him about the nice florist, the heavy statue, the flat tire, and how relieved we were that nothing had gotten broken. He listened intently, but didn't say much.

Entry # 7:

Now You See Me

or

How Sometimes You Can't See What's Right in Front of Your Face

When we got to the theater, Jordan parked away from the entrance in one of the darker sections of the parking lot. I asked him why we were parking so far from the theater's entrance, and he said he didn't want to get the doors on his truck scratched by kids opening their doors and banging the sides of his truck. We got out of the truck, and Jordan turned so he stood directly in front of me preventing me from going forward.

"Do you think I'm a fool?" he asked in a low

voice.

"No, of course not. Why do you ask that?"

"I saw you and Adam at school—and all the blankets comfortably arranged in his truck. You were talking, laughing, and carrying on about 'lover boy.' Were you talking about me? Laughing at me? Or if I'm out of sight, am I out of mind?" Jordan spat these words through clinched teeth, and then he added pointedly, "Did you think I wouldn't notice?"

"Notice what? I don't know what you are talking about. We just had to get the dumb statue and put it in the school. It was nothing," but I heard alarm in my voice.

I was frightened. I couldn't help it. I told myself to be calm, but I couldn't keep my hands from shaking.

"I don't believe it was nothing," Jordan continued. "You said you would be back by twelve. It was actually after three. What took so long? Did you stop for some private time?"

Before I could answer him, Jordan grabbed both of my shoulders and pinned me against the truck.

"You didn't have your necklace on when you were with Adam. I noticed. Was that your way of thinking you were free of me…that I wouldn't know?"

Instinctively, I grabbed for my necklace. I had put it on special for our date.

"Yeah," Jordan continued, "you have it on now, but why not then? I saw you parading in front of the whole basketball team. You can be so disrespectful… you make me furious."

He pushed me back into the closed door of the truck. As I steadied myself, I saw his hand rise, and before I could move, he slapped me across the jaw. I must have bit my tongue because I tasted blood. With both hands, he shoved me hard toward the front of the truck. Stumbling, I hit my forehead on the side mirror.

I grabbed the mirror for support, steadying myself in case another blow came, but Jordan stepped away.

He started pacing alongside the truck. Something told me not to speak. I ran my tongue around the inside of my cheek. I could feel a cut, and I tasted more blood. My tongue was swelling, and my head hurt. Several seconds passed in silence. I didn't move or say a word, but hot tears ran down my face.

"You just need to learn what is right," Jordan finally stated. "Now don't cry. You'll spoil our date."

Grabbing me by the arm, he led me toward the theater. I know I probably should have run or done something, but fear took control of me. Something kept telling me to lay low and play along—to not cause any more trouble. I don't remember buying the tickets, but I remember the previews had already started when we found our seats. The theater was dark, and I remember feeling grateful for the darkness.

Jordan watched the previews and the movie as if nothing peculiar had occurred. It was as if he had moved on. I couldn't. For the next two hours, I sat in the dark and took stock of what had happened.

What had I done? Nothing.

Why didn't he let me explain? He didn't want to hear my explanation.

Did he think I had to wear the necklace every minute? I had just left it off in the morning. I was saving it for our date.

Where had he been hiding at the school to see and overhear when we brought the statue back? I hadn't seen him.

Was he there just to watch me?

Did he watch me all the time?

The movie went by in a blur. I don't even remember what it was about. As the lights were brought up and we got up to leave, Jordan noticed the bruise on my forehead where I'd hit the mirror.

"I'm sorry you got hurt. I'll get some ice," he murmured.

When he walked toward the refreshment counter for the ice, I darted into the girl's bathroom. In the mirror, I saw a large bruise above my right eye. I hadn't paid much attention to it during the movie because I was so focused on the pain and swelling in my tongue.

I remember looking in that mirror at myself and trying to figure out what had happened. I prayed no one else came into the bathroom. My mind was racing, but my brain wasn't working. It was stuck in a loop between realizing it had happened again and wondering what I was going to do about it.

This time, though, I remember thinking, Jordan hadn't waited for an explanation. He didn't listen to me. He didn't want to hear what I had to say because he thought whatever I said wasn't true. It was disturbing the way he had just entered the movie theater like nothing happened. Was it my fault? I hadn't done anything. Had I?

I pulled a paper towel from the dispenser in the bathroom, wet it, and wiped my face. The cold water felt good on my forehead. In the mirror, my tongue looked black and blue. It was twice its normal size.

What was I going to do? I couldn't stay in the bathroom forever. I had to go out. I knew he'd be waiting.

Opening the door, I saw Jordan glancing anxiously up and down the hallway. He had a cup of ice in his hand, and when he saw me, he immediately rushed toward me.

"I was so worried about you," he cried out. "I thought you had left. I was scared. I didn't know where you were."

I just looked at him. I couldn't think of anything

to say, and my tongue didn't feel like engaging in conversation.

Gently Jordan placed the cup of ice on the bruise on my forehead. He put his other arm around my waist and guided me out the doors to the dark parking lot. Near his parked truck, he stopped.

"Look, Pepper, I'm sorry. I'm really sorry," he said. "I didn't mean to get so mad. I never wanted you to get hurt. When I couldn't find you just now, I was frantic. I was losing my mind—really. I love you. I don't know what I'd do if you left me. Life wouldn't be worth living without you."

I swallowed hard and tasted blood again. What was he saying? My mind was now in a dense fog, but I remember a few thoughts rising above the haze. Maybe they were fears. Was he talking about suicide? Would he really kill himself? What was I going to do? I needed time to think.

Finding my voice, I said simply, "I want to go home, Jordan. I'm tired, and I don't feel well."

I moved toward the truck, and Jordan opened the door. I had hardly sat down before he was behind the wheel. He started the engine, but we didn't move.

"Pepper, I am so sorry. So very sorry," he repeated. "Please don't leave me. I want you in my life. I can't imagine life without you. Give me another chance. I promise I'll make it up to you."

He sounded desperate. I knew he meant it, but he had meant it before in the hayfield, too. Yet, it had happened again…and this time was stranger than the first.

I had no idea what to say, but I knew I didn't want to say anything that might make him angry again.

"It's okay, Jordan," I finally mumbled over my swollen tongue. "I just want to go home and get some rest. It's been a long day."

He drove the truck out of the parking lot, and soon we were standing on the steps outside my front door.

"Tell me you love me, Pepper. I need to hear it."

There were tears in Jordan's eyes.

I honestly don't know what I felt right then, but a strong sense of self-preservation was taking hold. I just knew I didn't want to say anything that might upset or irritate him. All I could think of was to get safely inside my house.

"I love you, Jordan."

Quickly I opened the door, went inside, and turned to face him.

"Good night," I said automatically, and I shut the door.

Entry # 8:

The Silence of the Lambs

or

How a Secret Can Be Kept from Others in the Hope of Keeping It from Yourself

That night, I felt so mixed up. Fortunately, my parents were in bed, and I got to my room unnoticed. I knew I needed to think.

What had happened? Was it me? How does Jordan misunderstand what happens so badly? Am I that bad at communicating? Would he commit suicide?

Nothing made sense, and before I had any profound insight, I fell asleep.

The next morning, I woke to find Sage standing at the foot of my bed. I had forgotten we had made plans to go to church together. She was staring at me.

"What happened to your forehead?" Sage asked.

I couldn't lie to Sage, but I couldn't answer either. I just sat up on the side of the bed.

"What happened to your forehead?" she repeated.

I considered my options. I hadn't come up with any real answers on my own, but maybe Sage could. She was always good at giving advice, and I trusted her.

"If I tell you, Sage, will you promise me, swear to me, that you won't say anything?"

Sage paused and looked carefully at me, but she promised.

I tried to gather my thoughts into a coherent stream, but it was as if the faucet tap had been opened, and everything poured out in a gush. I had missed talking with Sage. I told her about the hayfield, the parking lot at the movies, and how Jordan could get so jealous. I told her I knew we should probably break up, but I was scared that if I brought up any kind of separation, it might make him worse. I wasn't sure what he would do if we stopped seeing each other—but it could be bad—he might hurt himself. He had even hinted at suicide. I admitted, too, that it might be me setting him off—triggering his anger. I told Sage that I was worried it might be my fault.

"Sometimes," I said, "I say something or do something that makes him so mad—so angry that he doesn't know what to do."

"So mad that he hits you?" Sage asked pointedly.

I tried to explain that it had only happened twice, and Jordan and I had been together on many, many occasions. For the most part, our time together was wonderful.

"I hope…I mean I think if I am careful about certain things, we can make it work. I believe I can get him to change. Jordan really is sorry. I mean he truly wants us to stay together. He wants it to work so badly. Sage, he says he loves me."

"Pepper, when people love you, they don't intentionally hurt you."

I didn't answer right away. I knew Sage was right, but I still didn't know what to do.

"Sage," I eventually said, "promise me you won't say anything to anyone. You have to keep it a secret. I'm not ready to talk about this. I've got to think, and right now, I've got to get dressed for church. I'll just tell people I hit my head on a cabinet door or something. Just don't tell anyone."

Sage nodded. I knew I could trust her to keep my secret.

I got dressed, and we left for church. Afterwards, we wanted to talk more, but neither of us knew exactly what to say. It was awkward to say the least. I didn't like feeling awkward around my best friend. Sage had to meet her family for dinner, and so did I, so we didn't have much time for conversation anyway, but the way I remember it, our conversation went something like this:

"Are you going to go to the Valentine's dance with Jordan on Saturday?" Sage asked.

"Cupid's Party Night," I remember groaning out the words. I had forgotten about it completely. "I guess. I mean I've already told Jordan I would, and I don't want to upset him. Besides, I don't know how I would tell him 'no' now. I'm not sure what he would do."

"What do you want to do?"

"I don't know," I answered, and it was the truth.

Sage stared at me. I felt like she was looking me over with a magnifying glass and clearly seeing every blemish and problem. Finally, she looked away, but she started talking again as if to herself.

"We have to figure something out, but for the life of me, I don't know what. I don't have any sage advice this time. I just know it isn't right. It isn't right."

Sage paused briefly, and then continued.

"I wish I didn't have to go, but my family is expecting me. I don't know what to say, Pepper, but for some reason I don't want to say good-bye."

Throwing up her hands in exasperation, Sage hugged me, and added, "Don't laugh, but all I can think of is 'Live long and prosper'."

We both managed a weak smile.

"Unfortunately, Sage, I'm not part of the *Star Trek* crew. I need advice in the here and now. Besides, I don't think even Spock could fix the mess I'm in."

"You're probably right," Sage answered. "It might take more emotional growth than Spock could muster. It may take more than we can muster."

We looked awkwardly at each other. Neither of us was used to being so uncomfortable.

"Promise me you won't say anything to anyone. It has to be our secret," I pleaded.

Sage nodded, but she still didn't move to leave. Solemnly, she held out her hand for our old "spice bump."

I instinctively responded with the same move.

"Spice Spirit?" Sage questioned.

"Spice Spirit," I responded.

We both smiled. We hadn't done our signature move in years. This time it wasn't accompanied with our customary, enthusiastic yell of "Spice Spirit," but as Sage finally walked away, I realized it still felt good. I think maybe we should resurrect the move—for private use only, of course—because there is no denying, as a pick-me-upper, it still has merit.

Sage and I talked a lot that week—whenever we got the chance. We considered and eliminated several courses of action regarding Cupid's Party Night. She brought up possible options, and I suggested excuses for not attending the dance. We both felt, however, that Jordan knew me and my schedule too well. He would question any deviation at this late date. Even if we did come up with a plausible excuse, there was no way to predict how he would respond. I feared it would be negative. It seemed like the best course was just to lay low, get through the Valentine's dance, and then gradually insert some space and distance between us.

I also did a lot of personal soul-searching during that week. I'm not a total idiot. I had heard about domestic violence and spousal abuse. I live in Missouri, not a third-world country. We have radios, televisions, and the internet! I had seen news reports about football players attacking their wives, dates, or whatever, but that was in the pros—the professional leagues—in the real world. This was high school, and this was my world.

Besides, I wasn't sure it was exactly the same thing. I mean I thought it might be, but Jordan and I weren't engaged or married. We were just a couple. My instincts told me we were a couple in need of separation. Perhaps that could be managed in time, but for now I just needed to deal with the rapidly approaching Cupid's Party Night. No matter how I added it up, I knew Jordan was expecting me to go to the dance with him. I couldn't see a way out of it.

Sage had made plans to attend the dance with Dillon, and on the Friday afternoon before the Saturday night dance, we sat in my room discussing scenarios. We finally decided it seemed best to try to arrange it so the four of us spent time together as much as possible—safety in numbers and all that. Everything might go alright if we made it more of a double-date outing, even though we would be driving to and from the dance separately.

I remember, as I got up to look out the window, it occurred to me I had not asked Sage for some time how things were going with Dillon.

"Are you and Dillon good? Are things working out between you two?"

"They're great—absolutely wonderful. Dillon is really a super guy. I'm kind of surprised how much I like him," Sage answered, but then she stopped abruptly.

I realized she didn't want to rave over Dillon when I was having so much trouble with Jordan. She seemed embarrassed by what she had already said.

"It's okay," I reassured her. "I'm glad it's working out for you two. I thought it would work out for Jordan and me, but I'm beginning to realize that maybe it was never meant to be."

There was silence for a minute or two, and then I noticed that Sage had drifted away.

"What are you thinking about?" I asked.

"One has got all the goodness, and the other all the appearance of it," she said softly.

I recognized that line. It was from our "Great Books" class.

"Jane Austen, *Pride and Prejudice*. Darcy and Wickham," I said. "I read that one, Sage."

"I read it, too, but it really didn't register at the time. It does now, though."

I could see what was taking hold in the depths of Sage's eyes. You couldn't miss it—the realization of what she was saying. Jordan had all the appearance of goodness, but it was Dillon who was actually good.

At some level, I think I knew Sage was right, but I wasn't ready to admit it. I was still bouncing between fear, frustration, and hope when it came to Jordan, so I punted.

"Sage, that line was written a million years ago. I mean we're talking about today—the here and now. I need help now!"

"I know, but it rings true even now. Austen did write

it a long time ago, but it is just as true now. I mean, in a way, it is kind of comforting."

"How?" I asked bluntly.

"Well, it means people were having trouble figuring out other people a long time ago. I mean people have been having relationship problems for hundreds of years. Maybe not exactly like us, but in some ways exactly like us."

"And how is that comforting to me?"

"It means…it means we're not alone. Everyone is messed up in one way or the other, and it takes a long time to figure other people out."

I looked at Sage carefully. Once again, she was right.

Maybe Sage is becoming wiser and more of a real philosopher. Perhaps her parents did know what they were doing when they named her Sage. I mean maybe they were thinking about more than the spice…the herb…or whatever.

Entry # 9:

Saturday Night Fever

or

How Cupid Can Misfire and Hit You in the Head Instead of the Heart

The following evening Jordan arrived to take me to Cupid's Party Night. He looked wonderful, and he was as polite and sweet as he could be. He told me several times how great I looked, and I began to feel that everything would be okay. I can get through this I told myself.

As soon as we arrived at the school, I made sure we found Sage and Dillon. Everyone was there, and from all appearances, the dance was a big success. The decorations were great, and there was a huge table of food with everything from heart-shaped pizzas and cut-out sandwiches to pink cookies and red cupcakes. The food committee had outdone themselves.

The Cupid statue Adam and I had set up was also proving to be a successful attraction. Everyone was stopping to take their selfie with the giant, white "god of love." The four of us even took turns taking pictures of ourselves with Cupid. In one, Sage and Dillon acted rather goofy, while Jordan and I were extremely formal. Then we switched, and Dillon and I acted crazy, while Sage and Jordan looked extremely serious. Some of our expressions and poses were horrible, and I remember thinking I hope none of these pictures make it into the yearbook.

Adam Ansley came up and commented that the two of us had done a good job. Cupid was proving to be popular, and in retrospect, he felt it was worth all the effort. I told him I agreed seeing as how everybody seemed to be enjoying it.

Dallas Freeman arrived carrying his cell phone. He wanted a picture of Adam and me beside the statue for the school newspaper. We posed as Dallas directed, but it made me nervous. I tried to see how Jordan was reacting to this, but he had walked away. I think he had gone to get a drink.

The rest of the night went by rather quickly. People danced, one of our choir groups sang, and a few kids from the drama department even performed a modern Romeo and Juliet-type skit. It was pretty funny. A few teachers even spoke about the dance and their past Valentine's Days. They were pretty hysterical in their own way, too. All in all, it was turning out to be a better-than-average high school dance.

There was only about a half hour left when Adam approached me and asked me to take a look at Cupid. I glanced at Jordan for, I guess, approval, but he just shrugged and walked away for another drink. So, I followed Adam.

When we arrived at the statue, Adam pointed to a crack in the long bow in Cupid's hand. We had promised the owners of the florist we would return Cupid safely, so I know Adam was concerned. Neither of us wanted to pay to fix this statue—no matter how successful Cupid proved to be.

"Do you remember seeing a crack there when we picked it up?" Adam asked.

"No," I answered. "Someone must have leaned on it tonight or pushed against it."

"I was afraid of that. I think it will hold," Adam said studying the injury. "I mean it doesn't seem cracked all the way through. It is more of a deep scratch, but we're going to have to be really careful getting him back. Be sure you bring all of those blankets for padding—and extras if you have any more. I'd really like to get this thing back without any major damage they can complain about or charge us for."

I promised I would bring all the padding I could find, and then I made my way back to Jordan. He was talking to Dillon and Sage. I tried to speak with him about the crack in the statue, but Jordan didn't want to talk. He said he just wanted to dance one last time before the music stopped and the school closed for the night. We danced the last dance in silence.

Entry # 10:

Fast and Furious

or

How in the Blink of an Eye You Can Lose Everything

Jordan and I were supposed to go out to eat with Sage and Dillon after Cupid's Party Night. When we left the gymnasium, I gathered up my coat and purse to head for his truck, but Jordan said he had to go to the boys' locker room to get something. Wrapping his arm around my shoulders, he asked me to walk down the hallway with him toward the football team's lockers.

At this point, my guard was up, but Jordan seemed okay. Maybe he was a little quieter than usual, but I supposed he might be tired. I was exhausted.

The overhead lights had been turned off in that part of the school, and it was only occasionally from the small security lamps that I got a glimpse of Jordan's face. Suddenly I realized his jaw was set tight and his eyes were staring intently straight ahead.

Jordan's facial expression immediately caused me to feel frightened. Something told me to run, but his strong arm on my shoulders, seemingly getting tighter with each step, made me feel that was not possible. When we rounded the corner toward the football team's lockers, it started.

Jordan turned and grabbed my face in his hands.

"What do you think you were doing taking pictures with Adam Ansley?" His hands were like ice, but his face was on fire.

"I wasn't doing anything. It didn't mean anything. I only did it because Dallas wanted a picture for the school paper."

"And you do whatever Dallas asks, don't you? Plus, you just couldn't wait to have more private time with Adam. That seemed like a pretty serious conversation the two of you were having earlier. You really enjoy being with him, don't you? The only thing you like more is flaunting it right in front of me. You go out of your way to taunt me," Jordan accused.

"No," I answered. I was intent on explaining this time. "We're responsible for that statue. Adam found a crack, and he was worried about it. He just wants to get it back safely. That was all—I swear it."

I don't think Jordan heard me because he continued as if I'd never spoken.

"You delight in trying to shame me in front of other people. You do it every chance you get. You need to learn," and with that his right hand flew at my head.

Pulling away, I fell back, so the blow only grazed my temple. Jordan's hand, however, banged hard into the metal lockers. He didn't yell, but he looked at me like it was my fault that he had missed his target. Rage filled his face, producing that expression I'd hoped I'd never see again. Before I could move or respond, he continued.

He hit me across the jaw, and I fell to the floor. Bending over my head, he started pummeling me with his fists. My forehead and right chest began to hurt. I tried to roll on my side to get out of his way. As I turned, he stood up and began kicking me on my left side. I couldn't exactly tell where the blows were coming from, but one particular kick on my left side caused immediate and severe pain in my left abdomen and shoulder.

I remember feeling seriously afraid. My vision began to blur, and I felt faint. I thought I was going to pass out right then, but I remember Jordan grabbing my neck with both hands. His knee was sticking into my chest, his face was inches from mine, and he was choking me. I couldn't breathe. I tried to tell him I couldn't breathe, but no words came out. I tried hard to inhale, but no air came. I was suffocating. Everything began to darken. I remember thinking, "I'm going to die." Don't laugh, because it definitely wasn't funny at the time, but the last thought I had before I passed out was that the Egyptians were often buried with their spices.

Entry # 11:

Awakenings

or

How to Climb Out of a Black Hole

It turned out that soon after I lost consciousness, Sage and Dillon arrived in the hallway. Sage later told me that she had been extremely worried throughout the dance. Call it intuition, or the "spice connection," but when Sage saw me leave the gym with Jordan, she convinced Dillon they should follow us. When they came upon us in the hallway and saw Jordan choking me, Dillon rushed over, grabbed Jordan, and knocked him to the ground. Sage dialed 911.

Paramedics took me to the hospital. When I woke

up, a nurse was standing by my bed. At first, I didn't remember what had happened. I asked her what was wrong with me, and she said I had been the victim of dating violence. The words hardly computed. I had never heard of "dating violence." Soon, Sage and my parents arrived. They told me how Dillon had stopped Jordan. Dillon saved my life.

Simply put, I never saw Jordan again. Not that I did or did not want to see him. It's just legally, partly because Sage and Dillon were witnesses, I got out of having to face him again. I did have to give my version of what happened to the authorities, but it turned out there was a school security camera (who knew?) in that hallway, so everything that happened was recorded on video. For me, the legal issues about what happened turned out to be easy. Unfortunately, it was not so easy to deal with my physical and emotional issues.

I was in the hospital for about a week. Along with the abrasions and contusions on my neck, chest, and sides, I also had a laryngeal fracture and severe swelling around my throat. For days, it was hard to swallow, and my voice sounded strange and raspy. I had three broken ribs and a ruptured spleen. Did you know you can live without a spleen? I found out you can because they had to take mine out. It was bleeding so badly the doctors had to remove it. My recovery was a rather rocky road, but in the ensuing few weeks, I healed physically. The road to mental and emotional health took a little longer.

The medical doctors had a psychologist come to visit me while I was in the hospital. I learned from him that when people truly fear for their life or think they are going to die, it is not uncommon to recall things related to death—something they've heard, feared, or associated with dying. Leave it to me to think about the

Egyptians and their spices!

The major benefit of the psychologist's visits, however, was that he had a female therapist who worked with him. She came to see me often—even after I got out of the hospital. As fate would have it, her name was Ginger! It seems life is full of spice; you just have to keep looking.

Entry # 12:

Back to the Future

or

How When You're on a Journey, You Should Look Back to See How Far You've Come

Ginger is the therapist who recommended I write this diary. I guess she was right because I think writing everything down has helped. I've met with Ginger weekly, and we've talked about each of my diary entries. Our conversations have been good, and I feel like I have learned a lot about myself, about dating violence, and about partner abuse.

During our meetings, Ginger and I spent a lot of time talking about the roles people play in relationships and how relationships can deteriorate. There can be verbal, emotional, physical, and sexual abuse between partners. Some relationships benefit from counseling and problem solving solutions, but other victims need immediate exit strategies.

One thing I learned from Ginger is that for many victims the aggression doesn't progress as rapidly as it did with me. For some, it often begins with name calling, but referring to a partner as "fat," "ugly," or "stupid" is not normal or okay. It's demeaning and shows a lack of respect. Some people are involved for years with their partners as the verbal abuse, mental control, and physical attacks steadily progress and escalate. I guess I was lucky in that regard—because Jordan and I were only together for a few months.

I also learned that many cases of dating violence are never reported to the authorities. Victims are often silenced by cultural or social customs. Sometimes victims don't seek help because of fear of retaliation from their attackers, but seeking help is important. Silence gets you nowhere, and secrets can kill.

From Ginger, I also learned that abusive relationships happen a lot more often than you might think. Ginger says some studies estimate one in three adolescents has been in a dating relationship that became abusive—by either verbal, emotional, physical, or sexual means. It can occur in any type of relationship, and girls can abuse their boyfriends, too. It's a huge problem, and looking back, I wish I had known more about it earlier.

Above all, Ginger has taught me that people can't fix other people. Each individual is responsible for his or her own behavior. The blame wasn't with me—even though at the time I thought (feared?) it might be. You can make someone mad, but it's their responsibility to control their actions when they are angry.

I know I am much better, but sometimes my brain

still asks "Why me?" Ginger says there is no answer to that question. Dating violence or partner abuse can happen to anyone.

Some people who know my story say I should just forget all the bad that has happened and move on. I live in a small town, as I said, and everybody knows everything that happens to every person here. I can't forget, though, and the truth is I don't want to. I'm going to remember and learn from it.

I've learned I was wrong about Jordan. I thought he loved me, but he almost killed me. I thought I could fix everything, but people have to "fix" themselves. I was wrong about Dillon, too. I thought he was somewhat of a misfit, but he has proved, through all of this, to be a true friend.

Did I mention that Sage came to one of my meetings

with Ginger? It was no surprise to me that we all hit it off tremendously. After all, the three of us share the spice bond.

Sage mentioned during the session that she had taken to calling Dillon by the shorter version of his name—just Dill.

"Dill has just been great through this whole thing," she confided to us.

"Dill?" I asked.

"Yes, I call him Dill now instead of Dillon. He likes it," Sage grinned.

"You do know that dill is a spice?"

"Of course, I know. He's one of us."

We all laughed, and it felt good to laugh again. One thing I have learned for certain through all of this is that it is friends who are the true spice of life.

During that meeting with Ginger and Sage, I remember Sage repeating her line about how it takes time to figure people out—to tell the good guys from the bad guys.

"You're right as usual, Sage," I said, "but I might add that it takes time to figure yourself out, too. I mean to figure out what you really want, what you need, and what makes you happy."

"You know," Sage said, "you've been hanging around me too long. You're starting to sound like the sage!"

The truth is I don't know if I'm really any smarter or not—but I'm trying. I do know Sage was right about it being a strange and funny world. Well, maybe I should say her country song was right. I mean it is kind of strange and crazy that you almost have to die to realize how much you want to live.

This is my last entry in this diary. I want to get ready for my senior year and whatever comes after.

It has been estimated in the United States that approximately 1.5 million high school students experience physical abuse from a dating partner annually. Over 80% of parents, however, don't think dating violence is an issue or are not aware of it as a problem. Beyond the physical abuse, many victims may also experience verbal, emotional, and sexual abuse.

Billie Holladay Skelley is a registered nurse who received her bachelor's and master's degrees from the University of Wisconsin in Madison. As a nurse, she recognizes that middle grade and high school students face many dating issues and partner concerns, and she hopes this text will foster further discussions regarding what actions are acceptable and what behaviors are not acceptable in positive relationships. She hopes *Spice Secret: A Cautionary Diary* will spread awareness and help to stop dating abuse before it starts!

www.ingramcontent.com/pod-product-compliance
Lightning Source LLC
LaVergne TN
LVHW050025080526
838202LV00069B/6915